W9-CAP-521

WITHDRAWN

CHARLESTON COUNTY LIBRARY

The Phone Booth in Mr. Hirota's Garden

Heather Smith

illustrated by
Rachel Wada

ORCA BOOK PUBLISHERS

EVERY MORNING Makio visited his neighbor, Mr. Hirota. Together they sat at the edge of his garden, looking down at the small figures on the harbor. They made a game of spotting Makio's dad as he unloaded the morning catch, and Mr. Hirota's daughter, Fumika, as she cleaned and gutted the fish.

"I see them!" Makio would say.

Mr. Hirota would laugh. "You win again, Makio."

It was one of their favorite games.

They were playing it when the shaking started and the big wave came.

Makio's father loved the ocean. He'd say, "Listen, Makio, the ocean is saying good morning."

The lapping waves would whisper:

O-hi-o.

   O-hi-o.

    O-hi-o.

Makio always returned the greeting.

Ohayo gozaimasu, ocean.

But on the day the big wave came, the ocean didn't whisper.

It roared.

Makio watched as the wave got bigger
and bigger.

"Oh, oh, oh!" cried Mr. Hirota.

A big, watery hand swept into the harbor,
snatching everything—and everyone—
in its grasp.

It even took Makio's voice.

Everyone lost someone the day the big wave came.

Silence hung over the village like a dark, heavy cloud.

Then one day:

Rat-tat-tat.

Rrr-rrr-rr.

Thump, thump, thump.

Makio watched from his window.
Mr. Hirota was building something.
But what?

It was a phone booth, painted white and with many
panes of glass.

Mr. Hirota went inside.

His voice floated out.

Fumika? It's your father. I miss you.

Makio was confused.

Fumika had been snatched by the ocean.

Just like Makio's dad.

When Mr. Hirota left the booth, Makio crept inside.

An old-fashioned phone sat on a table.

It had no plugs or wires.

It was a phone connected to nowhere.

Mr. Hirota visited his phone booth every day.

Soon the other villagers did too.

Their voices floated on the wind.

Hello, cousin. Today I fixed the boat. I will fish again soon.

Hello, Mom. I planted a tree for you today. A maple. Your favorite.

Sister, how are you? I rode your bike today. It fits me now.

Hello, my love. I painted our bedroom your favorite shade of blue.

Makio went down to the harbor.

For the first time since the big wave came, he used his voice.

He screamed at the ocean.

"Bring our people back!"

The waves lapped gently.

O-hi-o.

   O-hi-o.

      O-hi-o.

Makio sighed and looked up.

Mr. Hirota's phone booth sat high on the hill like a lighthouse.

The climb back up the hill was tiring.

Makio was hot and sweaty.

The phone felt cool in his hand.

Dad?
It's me.
Can you hear me?
I yelled at the ocean.
It said good morning anyway.

Guess what?
I did really well on my math test.
The cherry blossoms are in full bloom. Everything's pink!
Mom painted your room your favorite shade of blue.

I miss you, Dad.

Every morning Makio looks down at the harbor.

When the ocean says good morning, Makio thinks of his dad. Someday he'll return the greeting. But for now he makes a game of spotting Mr. Hirota from high on the hill.

"I see you!" Makio calls.

Mr. Hirota smiles and waves.

It's one of their favorite games.

Author's Note

After the death of his cousin in 2010, a man named Itaru Sasaki built a phone booth in his garden as a way to deal with his grief. Although the phone was disconnected, Sasaki believed his words rode the wind to his loved one. A year later, when a tsunami struck his coastal town of Otsuchi, thousands of mourners flocked to the phone booth, longing to connect to their missing loved ones. When I heard the story of Itaru Sasaki's "phone of the wind," I was struck by the beauty of how a simple object—a disconnected phone—could help a grieving community heal. It was this sense of hope and resilience that inspired me to fictionalize the story for a young audience. I hope that, like Makio, readers will see that sometimes in sadness there is beauty. In this case, it is found within the walls of Mr. Hirota's phone booth.

To Itaru Sasaki
—H.S.

To Dad, resilient and strong like the waves.
And to Mom, whose love runs oceans deep.
—R.W.

Text copyright © 2019 Heather Smith
Illustrations copyright © 2019 Rachel Wada

All rights reserved. No part of this publication may be reproduced or transmitted in any form or by any means, electronic or mechanical, including photocopying, recording or by any information storage and retrieval system now known or to be invented, without permission in writing from the publisher.

Cataloguing in Publication information is available from Library and Archives Canada

Issued in print and electronic formats.
ISBN 9781459821033 (hardcover) | ISBN 9781459821040 (PDF) | ISBN 9781459821057 (EPUB)

Library of Congress Control Number: 2019934057
Simultaneously published in Canada and the United States in 2019

Summary: This gorgeously illustrated picture book tells the story of a young Japanese boy who loses his dad in a tsunami.

Orca Book Publishers is committed to reducing the consumption of nonrenewable resources in the making of our books. We make every effort to use materials that support a sustainable future.

Orca Book Publishers gratefully acknowledges the support for its publishing programs provided by the following agencies: the Government of Canada, the Canada Council for the Arts and the Province of British Columbia through the BC Arts Council and the Book Publishing Tax Credit.

Inspired by traditional Japanese techniques, the artwork was created using watercolors, black ink and pencils, and assembled digitally.

Photograph of Itaru Sasaki's phone booth by Alessia Cerantola/BBC
Cover and interior artwork by Rachel Wada
Author photo by Declan Flynn
Illustrator photo by Sanna Woo
Design by Teresa Bubela
Edited by Liz Kemp

ORCA BOOK PUBLISHERS
orcabook.com

Printed and bound in China.

22 21 20 19 • 4 3 2 1